*To Roy, for help and sympathy
when the computer goes wrong!*
~ C F

*To Mom, Dad, Rach, Tim, Ange
and the rest of the back-up!*
~ L H

MGR PUBLISHING
4953 Dundas Street, W. Suite 105,
Toronto, Ontario, M9A 1B6, Canada

This edition produced 2005 for MGR Publishing
by LITTLE TIGER PRESS
An imprint of Magi Publications
1 The Coda Centre, 189 Munster Road
London SW6 6AW, UK
www.littletigerpress.com

Originally published in Great Britain 2005 by Little Tiger Press, London

Text copyright © Claire Freedman 2005
Illustrations copyright © Louise Ho 2005

All rights reserved • ISBN 1 84506 168 3

Printed in Singapore by Tien Wah Press Pte.

10 9 8 7 6 5 4 3 2 1

One Magical Morning

Claire Freedman

Louise Ho

In the shadowy woods,
one clear summer's morning,
Mommy took Little Bear
to see the day dawning.

The bears walked together
through grass drenched with dew.
Little Bear skipped,
as little bears do.

Little Bear gazed
as the sunrise unfurled.
"Up here," he cried,
"you can see the whole world!"

As the silvery moon
faded high in the sky,
Twinkle-eyed voles
came scurrying by.

And a little mouse gazed
as the morning sun
Melted the stars away,
one by one.

Fox cubs played while
the mist swirled like smoke,
Wrapping the trees
in its wispy cloak.

A pigeon coo-cooed
from a branch way up high.
Little Bear laughed,
"Look at me! Watch me fly!"

They stopped for a drink
at a babbling stream,
And the sun turned the forest
soft pink, gold and green.

Bushy-tailed squirrels
scampered down trees,
Hunting for pine cones
hidden by leaves.

"Look, Mommy!" cried
Little Bear in delight,
As a mole burst, blinking,
into the light.

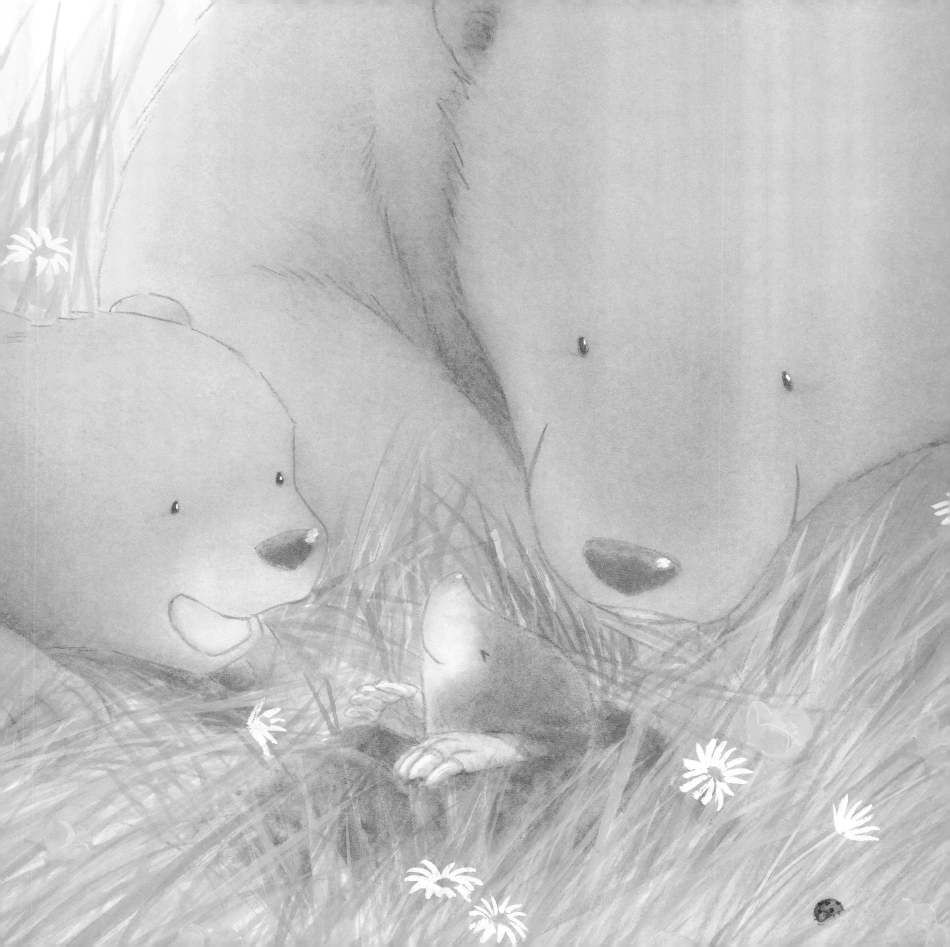

Mommy Bear smiled,
"Over here, take a peep!"
Bear's friend, Little Rabbit,
lay curled up asleep.

"Wake up, Little Rabbit,
come and play in the sun.
It's a beautiful day –
and it's just begun!"